To: Isabella and Kinley,

make sure every day is cheeky and full of adventure!

Tammi Titus

Robin Cheeky
and the MagicalSmileys

by Tammi Titus
Illustrated by Ross Chirico

 BRILLIANCE
PUBLISHING

Robin Cheeky and the Magical Smileys by Tammi Titus
Illustrated by Ross Chirico

ISBN: 978-0-9826743-0-7 (hard cover)
Library of Congress Catalog number: 2010902932

10 9 8 7 6 5 4 3 2

Printed and bound in the USA, February 2012

Published by Brilliance Publishing
PO Box 52 Cumberland RI 02864
Web site: www.BrilliancePublishing.com

Book Design by Jill Ronsley, Sun Editing & Book Design, www.suneditwrite.com

"I want to invite my friends over to play with me," says Robin Cheeky, "but my room is boring and plain. I need to make it exciting."

Robin Cheeky's fuzzy, rainbow colored cat, Pluxie, flicks her tail beside him. Then, Robin Cheeky's eyes light up and his cheeks turn cheeky-pink. "I know what to do. I'll draw smiley faces on the wall," says Robin.

Robin opens his roll-top desk and takes out his box of magical markers.

He picks only happy colors—
red, orange, pink, purple, blue and green.

He leaves the sad colors like black,
brown and grey in the box.

Robin Cheeky needs Pluxie's help because she has two tails,
so she can make smileys quickly.

"One smiley, two smileys, three smileys …" Robin counts.

Before they know it, every wall in the room is covered with smiley faces.

That night, Robin Cheeky's mom and dad come in to tuck him and Pluxie in. Robin notices their long faces.

"Robin, you must paint over the smileys," says Mom.

"Boo Hoo! Hoo! Hoo!" he cries.

Pluxie licks the teardrops that roll down Robin Cheeky's face.
The salty tears make her thirsty.
She runs for a drink from the water bucket.

"Meow! Meow!"

Robin Cheeky runs to Pluxie to see what happened.

"Boo Hoo! Hoo! Hoo!" he cries again.

Pluxie has fallen into the bucket, and all her rainbow colors have been washed away. She is just a grey and black cat.

"You are still my favorite cat, Pluxie, no matter what color you are," says Robin Cheeky. Pluxie licks Robin's hand and purrs.

Robin Cheeky and his cat get back to work. They cover the wall with a coat of white paint—but nothing changes. The smileys shine through! They paint another coat, and another, but the smileys keep shining through the paint.

"Pluxie," says Robin Cheeky, "our magical smileys are brighter and more sparkly than they were before we painted the wall white."

But Pluxie's rainbow colors do not return to her fur. The colors gave her the power to fly, and without them, she and Robin Cheeky would not be able to soar through the sky and travel the world on adventures.

Pluxie jumps onto Robin Cheeky's bed, lies at the end and puts her head down. Robin knows she misses her colorful coat.

"Pluxie," says Robin Cheeky, "I promise that
I will get your colors back—no matter what it takes!

I remember a story told by my grandfather. A wondrous world opened up every time he went to sleep. It was called the magical dream world. To enter the magical dream world, I must read before I go to sleep."

Robin Cheeky takes a book off the shelf, gets into bed and begins to read. While reading, he falls asleep and fades into the magical dream world.

So begins the adventure of how Robin Cheeky brings Pluxie's rainbow colors back.